This book belongs to

Copyright © 2014

make believe ideas ltd

The Wilderness, Berkhamsted, Hertfordshire, HP4 2AZ, UK.
501 Nelson Place, P.O. Box 14100, Nashville, TN 37214-1000, USA.

Illustrated by Kate Toms.
Designed by Charlotte Leigh and Annie Simpson.

The Twelve Days of Christmas

Kate Toms

make believe ideas

1 2 3 4 5 6

On the 1st day of Christmas,
my true love sent to me . . .

7 8 9 10 11 12

a partridge
in a pear tree.

On the **2**nd day of Christmas,
my **true love** sent to me . . .

On the **3**rd day of Christmas, my **true love** sent to me . . .

3 French hens,

2 turtledoves,

and a partridge in a pear tree.

2 turtledoves,

3 French hens,

and a partridge in a pear tree.

On the 5th day of Christmas,
my true love
sent to me . . .

5 gold rings,

Gold Rings

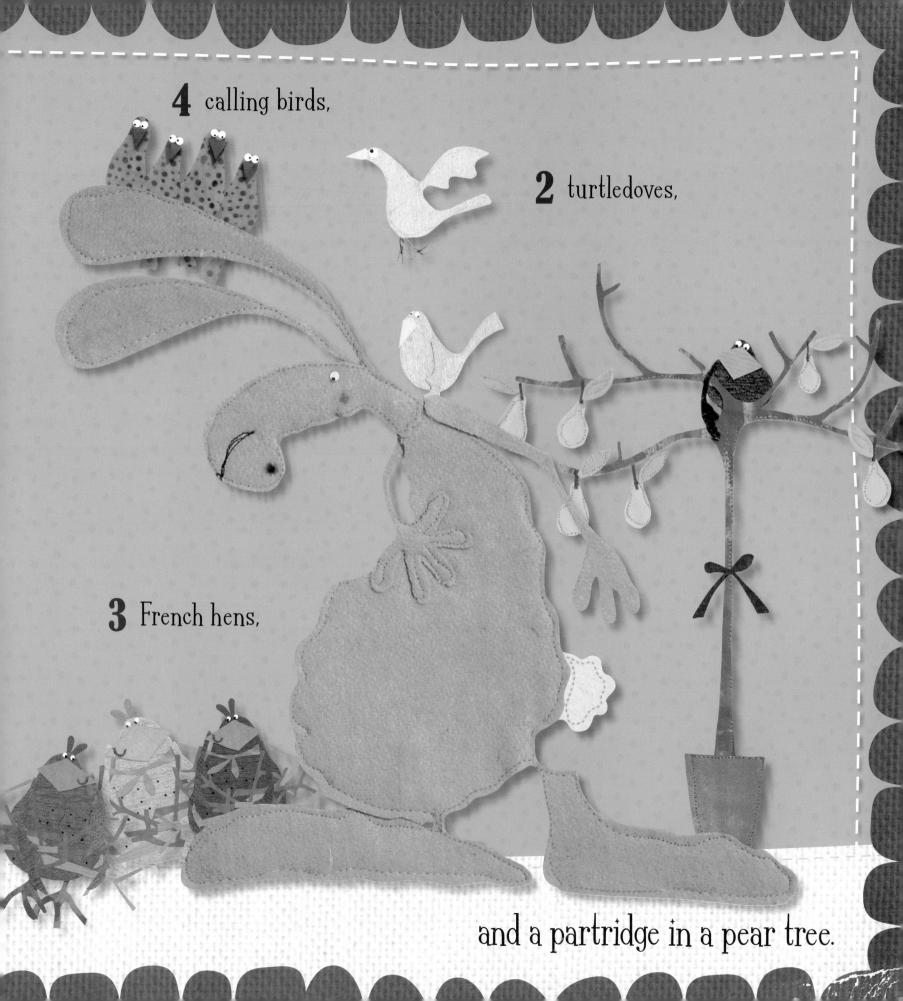

4 calling birds,

2 turtledoves,

3 French hens,

and a partridge in a pear tree.

On the **6**th day of Christmas, my **true** love sent to me . . .

5 gold rings, **4** calling birds, **3** French hens, **2** turtledoves,

6 geese-a-laying,

and a partridge in a pear tree.

squawk!

On the **7**th day of Christmas,
my true love sent to me . . . .

7 swans-a-swimming,

6 geese-a-laying, **5** gold rings, **4** calling birds, **3** French hens, **2** turtledoves,

and a partridge in a pear tree.

squawk!

On the **8**th day of Christmas, my true love sent to me . . .

7 swans-a-swimming, **6** geese-a-laying, **5** gold rings,
4 calling birds, **3** French hens, **2** turtledoves,

8 maids-a-milking,

squawk!

and a partridge in a pear tree.

On the **9**th day of Christmas,
my true love sent to me . . . .

8 maids-a-milking, **7** swans-a-swimming, **6** geese-a-laying,
5 gold rings, **4** calling birds, **3** French hens, **2** turtledoves,

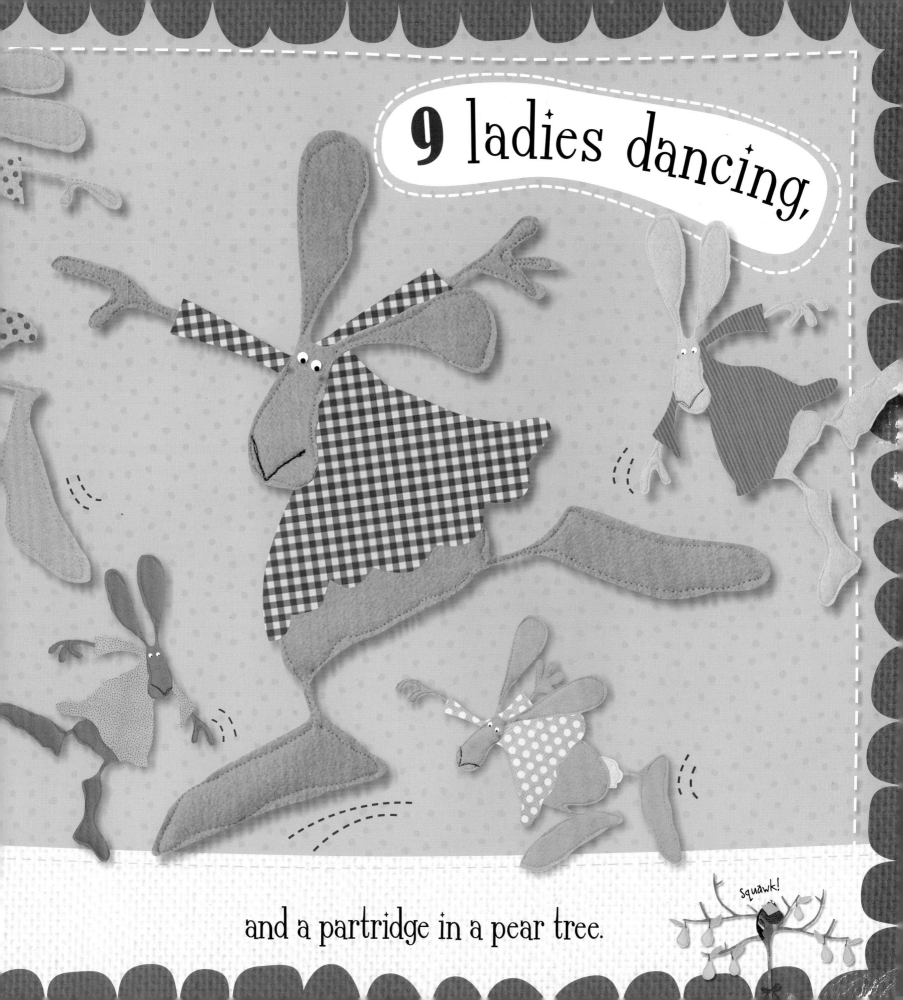

9 ladies dancing,

and a partridge in a pear tree.

squawk!

On the **10**th day of Christmas,

my **true** love sent to me . . .

9 ladies dancing, **8** maids-a-milking, **7** swans-a-swimming,
6 geese-a-laying, **5** gold rings, **4** calling birds, **3** French hens, **2** turtledoves,

10 lords-a-leaping,

and a partridge in a pear tree.

squawk!

On the **11**th day of Christmas,

my true love

sent to me . . .

10 lords-a-leaping, **9** ladies dancing, **8** maids-a-milking, **7** swans-a-swimming,
6 geese-a-laying, **5** gold rings, **4** calling birds, **3** French hens, **2** turtledoves,

On the **12**th day of Christmas, my true love sent to me . . . .

12 drummers drumming,

11 pipers piping, **10** lords-a-leaping, **9** ladies dancing, **8** maids-a-milking, **7** swans-a-swimming,

6 geese-a-laying, **5** gold rings, **4** calling birds, **3** French hens, **2** turtledoves, . . .

. . . . and a partridge in a pear tree.